Lana Rayberg. *Alonka and the Dinosaur*

ISBN 978-1-960533-87-6

Text and Illustrations by Lana Rayberg © 2025

Published by M·GRAPHICS | Boston, MA

　www.mgraphics-books.com
　mgraphics.books@gmail.com

Printed in the USA

Once upon a time there lived a girl. Her name was Alonka. She loves animals, but most of all she loves dinosaurs. She understands that she will never see living dinosaurs, and that makes her sad. She knows all types of those creatures, how they looked like and what they ate.

She also likes to study all kinds of animals, insects, snakes and birds. Alonka had a lot of toys, mostly animals, and no dolls. The best present on her birthday was not a Barbie Doll, not a book with sweet princess stories, but an Encyclopedia.

Every school day she left her plastic dinosaurs, snakes and lizards at home. She missed them all day long.

At school Alonka had a hard time in writing. She liked to write imaginative stories, but the teacher demanded that she create a realistic one. Mrs. Glitter keep saying, "Animals do not talk, and nothing magic happens. Write something what can REALLY happen in REAL life."

Alonka feel frustrated. She believed that animals talk and magic things do happen. She thought it was boring to write a story about a dentist visit or about a field trip. She enjoyed using her imagination.

sun
1+6=7
REAL!
• FIELD
TRIP
• DANT

Alonka spend every summer in Cape Cod, where her grandma lives. She feels happier there then in Brooklyn, because there was more space and no homework. Also, she can see different animals there, not only squirrels or rats. Alonka fed chipmunks, skunks, birds and wild cats. In the backyard she even saw a beautiful red fox. But Alonka felt lonely. She needed a friend. Kids did not want to play with her, because she talks only about dinosaurs.

"Why did they disappear? What happened to them?" She wondered one nice sunny day as she walked near the ocean and kicked small rocks with her foot. Suddenly, she kicked something very hard. Alonka looked closely at the rock and realized that it was a giant egg!

The Egg was very heavy. Alonka helds it with both hands. She carried the egg to the backyard and hid it under the wooden bench. Grandma was taking a nap on the terrace.

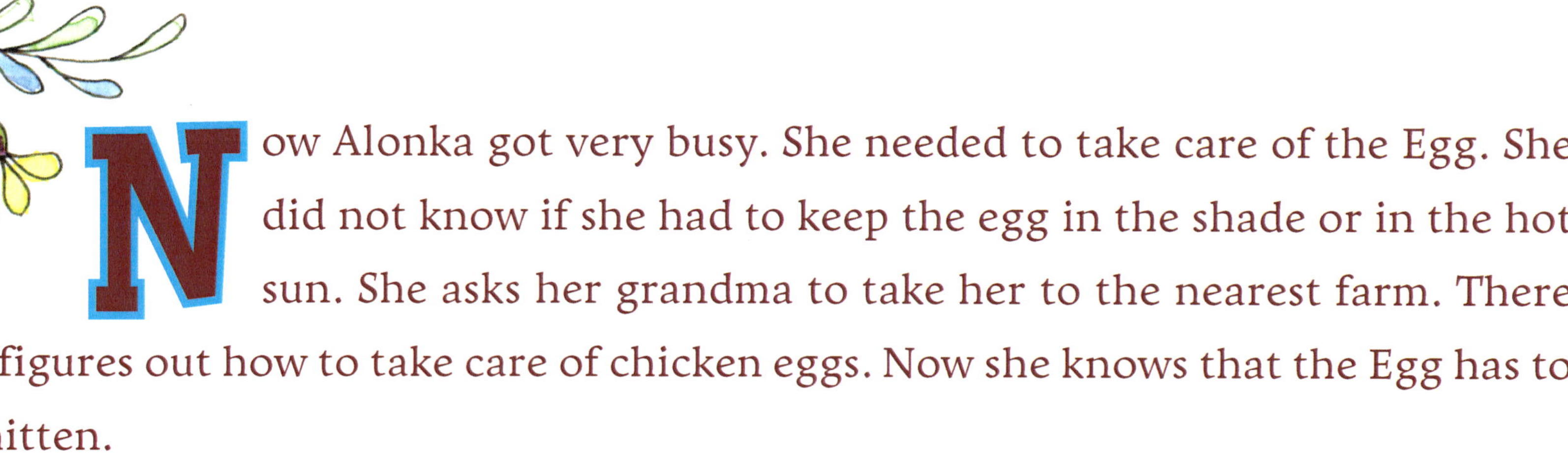

Now Alonka got very busy. She needed to take care of the Egg. She did not know if she had to keep the egg in the shade or in the hot sun. She asks her grandma to take her to the nearest farm. There she figures out how to take care of chicken eggs. Now she knows that the Egg has to be hitten.

Alonka covers the Egg with her winter coat at night, and during the daytime she rolls it under the bench and leaves it under the sun.

A few days pass by. Alonka sits near the Egg and looks at its lovely brown spots. Suddenly she hears a cracking sound.

"Crack! Crack!"

She sees a tiny piece of the egg shell break off. Alonka moved closer to the Egg and listens to the unknown creature knocked inside. Finally, after one more strong crack, a little head on a long neck popes out.

"Hello!" smiled Alonka.

"Hello!" agreed the creature. Then the head asked, "Where is my Mom?"

"I will be your Mom!" Alonka responds.

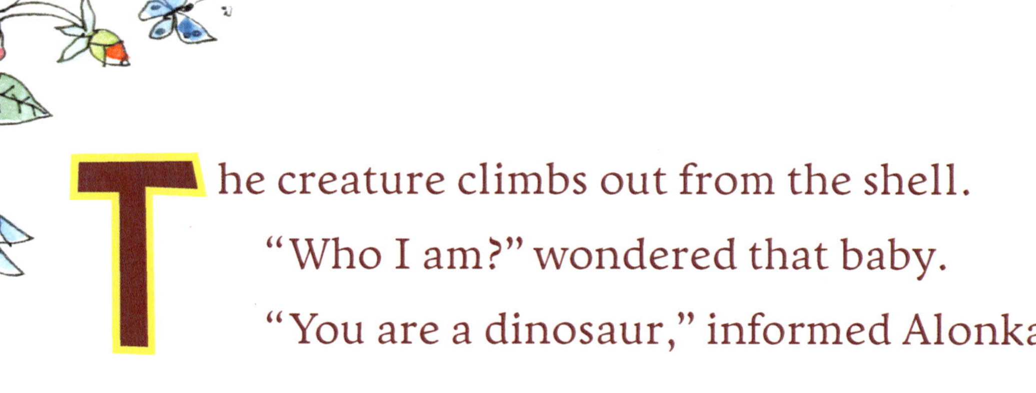

The creature climbs out from the shell.

"Who I am?" wondered that baby.

"You are a dinosaur," informed Alonka.

Alonka and dinosaur became friends. Alonka was not lonely any more. She was very busy.

First, she feels responsible for her pet. She feeds the dinosaur, and made sure it slept well.

Secondly, she keeps it a secret from everyone that she has a living dinosaur. Alonka was afraid, that adults might send him to the zoo.

In the little cottage where her grandma keeps the shovel, the broom, and other tools, Alonka made a cozy little bed for a Dino.

She spends all her spare time with her new friend. Mostly they played in the small garden in the backyard. Sometime they even come to the terrace when grandma took an afternoon nap. On the terrace Alonka and Dino played chess and enjoyed their tea ceremony.

ino grows and grows. Soon his tail did not fit in the cottage. "Why you are so big?" wondered Alonka. "You should be smaller!" Dino feels guilty, but could not stop to growing.

It was one problem.

Another problem was how to get enough food for a Dino. He ate all apples, leaves and even flowers from Grandma beloved rose garden.

Grandma become curious about how the leaves, red apples and the flowers have been disappearing.

"Did we have a hurricane?" She asks the neighbor.

"No", the neighbor was surprised. "We haven't had anything unusual."

"Xmmm…" murmured Grandma. "I guess, a group of birds came and ate everything. I should place a scarecrow in the garden to keep them away. But first I need to figure out who damaged the plants."

The next evening Grandma prepared to be a detective. During the day she took a long nap, then she packed up. She put a strong flashlight, thermos with hot tea and a couple of sandwiches in the plastic bag. Later in the evening Grandma changed her casual outfit into a sports suit. She also wore sneakers instead of sandals.

Grandma looks in Alonka's bedroom. The girl was sleeping. Actually Alonka did not sleep. She pretending to sleep. Every day after a goodnight kiss she sneaks outside and frees her dinosaur. So Alonka follows her usual routine.

She lets dino out of the broom cabinet. Dino was so happy! Almost all day long he is alone, except for the time when Grandma took her afternoon nap.

First dino puts Alonka on his back and gives her a ride. Alonka laughs from excitement. She grabs a few last apples from the top of an apple trees.
She eats one, and her friend eats the rest.

hen dino starts picking apples from the neighbor's garden over the gate.
Suddenly bright light sparks in their eyes. "Alonka! What's going on here?"
cries the Grandma. In a couple of minutes, the three of them sit on the
terrace and hold a meeting.

Alonka introduces the dinosaur to her Grandma. Dino apologizes to Grandma for eating all of her favorite flowers and fruits.

Grandma says, "You are such a nice polite guy. Thank you for keeping company for my granddaughter. You cannot live as a prisoner. I will introduce you to our community. But, by the way, do you have a name?"

"No."

"E very person should have a name," declared Grandma.

"I am Mrs. Polly, this is Alonka, and you are...

What name would you like to be called?"

"Fillip," replies dino shyly.

The next morning Mrs. Polly, Alonka and Fillip went shopping. Grandma introduced the dinosaur to everyone in the village. Fillip was shy, but he tried to be brave. He shook all the villagers' hands and politely said, "Hello!" Mrs. Polly tells her neighbors about the problem of feeding their friend.

So, the villagers offer to help in any way they can.

Mr. Brick, the bakery owner, gave them a few poppy seeds bread loaves, still warm.

Mrs. Vine presented a big jar of milk and a head of cheese.

Mr. Secret spears a basket of fruits and vegetables.

When they returned home, they enjoyed a big dinner. Alonka was so happy that she no longer needed to hide her Filip any more. Mrs. Polly was happy that her granddaughter has a friend. But Fillip looks concerned.

"Why do I look so different?" He asked suddenly. "We are human, and you are an animal," explains Mrs. Polly. "People can be friends with animals," added Alonka.

"I would like to find same creature that looks like me," tells Fillip.

"You will not find any!" cries Alonka. "Dinosaurs disappeared a long time ago!"

"Well, then I can meet other animals!" guessed Fillip. "I would like to live in the forest. There is more space and food for me, and I will be more independent."

"What about me?" shouts Alonka. "I need you! You are my friend!"

"Well, I will visit you. I will not go too far away and will return each summer."

Fillip does not want to wait until the next day. He decided to leave at once. Mrs. Polly packs up Alonka's school bag for him. She fills it with couple of sandwiches, a bottle of milk and a few boiled eggs. Alonka add to it her drawings and her favorite toy—a little plastic dinosaur.

Filip asks them for a matches and a flashlight. "Maybe I will need it for the first time," he suggests.

The three of them went outside of the village. Then they hugged each other. Alonka was very sad, but she tries not to cry. She understands that it will be better for a dinosaur to live in nature. Also, she hopes to see him often.

Alonka and Mrs. Polly stand and watch as Fillip walks away. Finally, he disappears between the trees.

"I will be back!" The echo brings his cheerful voice.

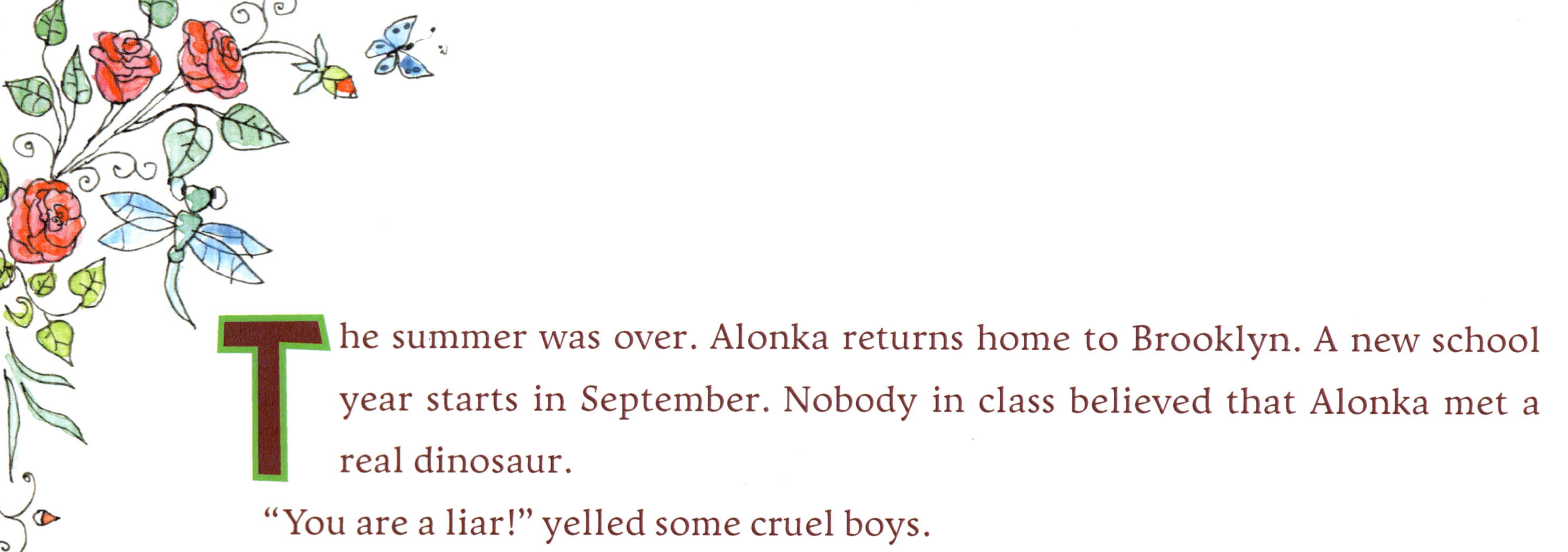

The summer was over. Alonka returns home to Brooklyn. A new school year starts in September. Nobody in class believed that Alonka met a real dinosaur.

"You are a liar!" yelled some cruel boys.

"Not, I am not!" protested Alonka.

The next day Alonka decided to bring a picture of herself, Grandma and Filip to school. Mrs. Glitter hung up the photograph on the chalkboard. Finally, she agreed that magic things happen.

Alonka become a very popular girl at school. She has friends and was not bored any more. But she missed her dinosaur and she could not wait until next summer. She knew that she will see him again.

Special thanks to

Andrei Bouzikov

Angela Kasserly

Michi Raab